SMURF SALAD

Peyo

SMURF SALAD

A SMURFS GRAPHIC NOVEL BY Peyo

WITH THE COLLABORATION OF
LUC PARTHOENS AND THIERRY CULLIFORD – SCRIPT
LUDO BORECKI AND JEROEN DE CONINCK – ART
NINE CULLIFORD – COLOR

PAPERCUTZ™
NEW YORK

SMURFS GRAPHIC NOVELS AVAILABLE FROM PAPERCUTZ™

THE SMURFS graphic novels are available in paperback for $5.99 each and in hardcover for $10.99 each, except for THE SMURFS #21-#26, and THE VILLAGE BEHIND THE WALL, which are $7.99 each in paperback and $12.99 each in hardcover, at booksellers everywhere. THE SMURFS 3 IN 1 are in paperback only for $14.99 each. THE VILLAGE BEHIND THE WALL 2: THE BETRAYAL OF SMURFBLOSSOM is $12.99 each in hardcover only. You can also order online at papercutz.com. Or call 1-800-886-1223, Monday through Friday, 9 – 5 EST. MC, Visa, and AmEx accepted. To order by mail, please add $5.00 for postage and handling for first book ordered, $1.00 for each additional book and make check payable to NBM Publishing. Send to: Papercutz, 160 Broadway, Suite 700, East Wing, New York, NY 10038.

THE SMURFS graphic novels are also available digitally wherever e-books are sold.

PAPERCUTZ.COM

SMURF SALAD

SMURF™ © Peyo - 2019 - Licensed through Lafig Belgium - www.smurf.com

English translation copyright © 2019 by Papercutz.
All rights reserved.

"Smurf Salad"
  BY PEYO
  WITH THE COLLABORATION OF
  LUC PARTHOENS AND THIERRY CULLIFORD FOR THE SCRIPT
  LUDO BORECKI AND JEROEN DE CONINCK FOR ARTWORK
  NINE CULLIFORD FOR COLOR.

"The Aerosmurf"
  BY PEYO

Joe Johnson, SMURFLATIONS
Léa Zimmerman, SMURFIC DESIGN
Bryan Senka, LETTERING SMURF ("SMURF SALAD")
Janice Chiang, LETTERING SMURFETTE ("THE AEROSMURF")
Matt. Murray, SMURF CONSULTANT
Izzy Boyce-Blanchard, SMURF INTERN
Jeff Whitman, MANAGING SMURF
Jim Salicrup, SMURF-IN-CHIEF

HARDCOVER EDITION ISBN: 978-1-5458-0335-6
PAPERBACK EDITION ISBN: 978-1-5458-0358-5

PRINTED IN INDIA OCTOBER 2019

Papercutz books may be purchased for business or promotional use. For information on bulk purchases please contact Macmillan Corporate and Premium Sales Department at (800) 221-7945 x5442.

DISTRIBUTED BY MACMILLAN
FIRST PAPERCUTZ PRINTING

We're hungry! What's there to smurf?

?

What?! It's the same thing we had for lunch!

WHAT?! AGAIN?

No way! Out of the question!

We don't want any more of that horrible slop!

"Horrible slop"? A little dish I lovingly smurfed over for hours for you?

Smurf us something else! You're starving us!

?

Leave him to me!

What's all this fuss about?

It's Chef Smurf. Everything he's been making for us lately is DISGUSTING!

He's trying to poison us!

© Peyo

Oh, come now! Aren't you exaggerating a little?

You think so? Well, you have a taste then!

3

≥Sniff?!≤ Uh....

Ah! You see?!

Hmm! You got to admit your dish has a rather unasmurfing aroma, Chef Smurf!

I can't smurf anything about it, Papa Smurf! How do you want me to smurf a good meal with THIS?!

?

It's true. It's impossible to smurf anything whatsoever with such vegetables!

That's odd of Farmer Smurf! I'll go ask him for an explanation!

I don't understand a thing, Papa Smurf! I smurfed them all with love! They don't lack for water or sunshine, for smurf's sake!

© Peyo

Look! It's so sad seeing vegetables in this state!

I'll smurf a few plants to examine them!

4

Later, in Papa Smurf's laboratory...

This is a chance to use my new smurfoscope! With those two magnifying lenses, it lets me smurf the smallest things!

Hmm, interesting! It looks like miniature mushrooms are leeching off the plant and keeping it from smurfing normally!

That's the first time I've ever smurfed anything of the sort! I need the advice of a specialist!

Meanwhile, I have to smurf something to help Farmer Smurf!

A fertilizer to smurf the growth of the plants and a natural fungicide for the mushrooms!

Here, Farmer Smurf! Smurf these two solutions into your watering supply! But only a few drops!

Usually, I'd rather let nature do its smurf, but if it's for a good cause...

Later...

I'll be gone for a few days, so behave!

© Peyo

9

All right then, Papa Smurf did say: "Only a few drops!"

Let's hope that will smurf some effect!

⇒Psst!⇐ Farmer Smurf! Do you have a few minutes?

Uh... When will the vegetables you smurfed with Papa Smurf's solutions be ready?

Oh, that... you know how it's smurfs with vegetables! We got to wait a few days!

A FEW DAYS?! Why, that won't do at all!

?

You absolutely must smurf them as fast as possible! Look at what I got!

?

Change menus or you'd better smurf out!

Are you sure you smurfed enough solution on your vegetables?

?

I'm certain we must smurf more!

Hey! Papa Smurf said--

POP

© Peyo

6

10

11

HEY! IS ANYONE HERE?!

What's with all this mess? Where have they all gone?

Of course, my good little Smurfs must be smurfing on the dam!

Or on the bridge over the Smurf River! That must be it...

Alas, Papa Smurf's hopes are dashed...

So, the Smurfs aren't at the dam or the bridge, or even at the lake smurfing around being lazy. What could have happened?

Gargamel! That must be it! He must have smurfed a way to capture all the Smurfs!

But at Gargamel's...

I swear I'll get revenge on those cursed blue gnomes!

The problem is how do I trap those vermin without knowing the location of their village?

© Peyo

11

Well, no Smurfs here! Strange!

I'll continue my search tomorrow! It's getting late, and I'm hungry! I haven't smurfed anything since this morning!

Hey! Apparently Farmer Smurf has solved his vegetable problem!

Mmm... Not bad!

?

—CRAC

That noise! It's my little Smurfs coming back!

Nobody?! But I'm sure I heard smurfing! Anyone there?

Is that you, Papa Smurf?

Is it really you?

Who else would it be?

© Peyo

12

YIPPEE! Papa Smurf is back!

We're saved!

What a welcome! You're very kind! I'm happy to see you too!

CHOMP! CHOMP!

But tell me what smurfed here? Where have the others gone?

They've been smurf vegetabl First then nex that's when the Poet

Yes! And Hefty Smurf said we had to smurf him in the storeroom and then...

Uh, one at a time!

No, it as Brainy murf who said that! And...

Let's smurf inside, you can tell me this more calmly!

A few moments later...

So here goes, after we smurfed uh... a little... hmm!.... of your solution on Farmer Smurf's crops, the harvest was smurfly abundant...

© Peyo

13

"And the Smurfs ate their fill once again...

Aaah... That's what you call a real meal! Thanks, Chef Smurf!

Uh... Heh heh! It's nothing, my friends, nothing!

Greedy Smurf, how can you still eat after such a meal? Nobody smurfs sarsaparilla anymore anyways!

I love it! It's like a little dessert!

"But that evening...

HELP! HELP!
Chef Smurf!

BAM BAM BAM

?

There's a monster out there! It's enormous and completely green!

Enormous and completely green?!

What's smurfing? What's all the noise?

Sounds like someone smurfed someone!

It's Scaredy Smurf. He says he saw a monster!

?

It's true!

Ha ha ha! A monster! That's a good one!

It was in the little alley!

→YAWN!←... Go ahead, show us! Then we can smurf back to bed soon!

14

?!

Aaah... There! You see?

© Peyo

No! You're a liar! Poet Smurf doesn't look like a huge green zucchini!

Yes, he's got the same smurf as any Smurf!

If it's true, smurf us a poem so we'll see!

Oh, thou who... ⇒Sniff⇐ ... wert handsome, Now thou art ill-favored... ⇒Sniff⇐

Hey, it's true that, if you smurf your eyes, you'd think you were listening to a bad poem by Poet Smurf!

Well, what happened to you then?

I have no smurf! When I went to bed, the green pimple on my nose was itching me a lot...

I woke up soon after! My bed had gotten too small! So I went to smurf at myself in the mirror and saw this horrible face! I thought it was a nightmare and I smurfed out of my home! And that's when I ran into Scaredy Smurf!

But it wasn't a nightmare, and I've really become a monster!

Well, my smurfness! What a story!

Do you all think I'll stay like this forever? Farmer Smurf, you know about vegetables... What do you think?

I sure do know my vegetables, but I've never seen a zucchini smurf all by itself!

Papa Smurf will know better than me!

© Peyo

18

Hmm... If I may be allowed, I think I'm just as capable of smurfing this problem! And like Papa Smurf always says: "Never smurf off until tomorrow what you can--"

POW

We'll wait for Papa Smurf's return then!

The next day, the whole village was smurfed around Zucchini Smurf... uh... Poet Smurf!

"Some even used the opportunity to make fun of his smurf...

Poor Poet Smurf!

That's what smurfs when you want to be the top banana!

Jokey Smurf, that's not very smurf of you!

HA! HA! HA! HA!

It's true! Here... to apologize for myself! Don't worry, it's not a firesmurfer!

SPROTCH

© Peyo

I wanted to smurf some butter on the spinach! But I forgot you were a zucchini!

HA! HA! HA! HA!

17

EEEEEEEEK!

That's Smurfette!

She's in danger, for smurf's sake!

HOLD ON, SMURFETTE! WE'RE COMING!

There's a pickle in my laundry!

Who are you? Don't be afraid. Come out of there!

Yes, show your vegetable smurf!

?!

⇥Bwwaaaah!⇤ Smurf! I was s... of being sm... pickle, I ...

What's smurfing on here?

Jokey Smurf and Vanity Smurf have smurfed into vegetables!

There's three of them now!

Look at this horrible green tint and all these bumps on my smurf!

Bah! Smurf yourself in a little vinegar, and nobody'll notice! Whahaha!

This is getting worrisome! We got to smurf something!

Let's smurf a meeting!

© Peyo

19

"So, a meeting presided over by Hefty Smurf was smurfed...

Quiet, please! Quiet!

BLA BLA SMURF BLA

BLA BLA BLA

BLA BLA

BLA BL

BLA

BLA

BLA

I SAID QUIET!

Thank you! We've gathered here to smurf this problem preoccupying us, which you all know about!

Uh... I don't really see what you're smurfing about!

Dopey Smurf, you leave, or else we'll never get anything done!

!

Hey, can you smurf a little less loudly? I'm trying to sleep!

You too, Lazy Smurf. OUT!

Really! We're here to smurf serious things!

So then, can anyone explain what's happened to our three friends?

20

© Peyo

24

ME! I'd like to smurf something even if you never listen to what I smurf and, what's more, if Papa Smurf were here, it wouldn't smurf like that!

Could someone shut him up and smurf him outside?

But I think there's another question we should smurf!

That question is: "Why did they smurf one after the other and not all three at the same time?"

That's true! He's right for once!

Yesterday, Poet Smurf's the one who turned into a zucchini...

Yes, and today, Jokey Smurf and Vanity Smurf!

Maybe they're contagious!

CONTAGIOUS?!

© Peyo

21

Well... What then, my friends?

Don't come any closer, Jokey Smurf!

If you take another step, I'll smurf my smurf in your smurf!

?!

You might contaminate us! And we'd be smurfed into vegetables too!

Yes, we have to quarantine them!

WHAT?!

Quarantine us?

You don't have the right to smurf that! Papa Smurf is the village leader and he isn't here!

You're right, Jokey Smurf! So we'll smurf a vote by raising hands!

Don't worry! With all the friends we have, we have nothing to fear!

All those who agree they should be quarantined, smurf your hand!

I thought we had friends?

Uh...

22

© Peyo

26

"But the next morning, when I was smurfing their food...

I smurfed a bit of soup for you!

Heh heh! Surprise!

Hey, where has your guard Dopey Smurf smurfed?

?

Uh... Chef Smurf?

WHAAAH! A potato-smurf?

Something funny happened to me last night!

Help! He's been smurfed into a potato!

ZIP

Hey, wait!

He didn't give me time to smurf him what happened to me!

You'll have plenty of time to talk once you're with us!

With you? What do you mean?

Think, idiot! You've become a vegetable like us! What do you think they'll smurf to you? Make fries?

You... You think that --?!

No way, I don't want to be locked up with you!

© Peyo

"Unfortunately, it was only beginning...

I'm a cabbage! I'm a cabbage!

"Those who smurfed into vegetables were immediately hunted down...

"...and locked away with the others!

"Some smurfed masks to try to protect themselves from the illness...

"...But it was no use!

"The storeroom continued to fill!

Make room, please!

You pack of smurfs, you wait till we get out of here!

Hey! Take your hand away from there, if you don't want the back of mine upside your smurf!

"Until the day when it was Hefty Smurf's turn to be smurfed...

Oh, no!

"So we were the last four left!

© Peyo

27

31

Smurf them! Let them become monsters like us!

AAAAAH! I don't want to become a monster!

"So, we took refuge in the caves in the mountains..."

Since then, we've been smurfing to the village from time to time at night, waiting for your return!

And where are the other Smurfs now?

Uh... They smurfed into the forest, but we don't know where!

Hmmm... Okay! We'll see about that later! Let's smurf instead to the bottom of these transformations!

Let's start by going to smurf at your garden, Farmer Smurf!

Uh... now, Papa Smurf? ...In the dark of night?

The sun is up! Let's go!

Soon after...

It's just as I thought!

© Peyo

23

Farmer Smurf, I told you: "Only a few drops!"

I... I was pressured, Papa Smurf!

Pressured? By whom?

"..."

Chef Smurf! Can you please stay with us?!

Heh heh heh! Uh... →Gulp!←

So, it seems you influenced Farmer Smurf so he'd smurf more solution on his vegetables?

Ohh! He's exaggerating, Papa Smurf! It was just one or two extra drops!

One or two! Yeah, my smurf!

Just go ahead and say it's my fault!

It sure is!

That's enough! Now's not the time!

We'll resmurf this later! The important thing is to understand what happened to the others and find out how to cure them!

What's the connection with the garden?

I think eating these mutant vegetables is what smurfed the Smurfs!

© Peyo

30

What makes you believe that, Papa Smurf?

You four, for example! You haven't been smurfed! Have you eaten those vegetables? You, Farmer Smurf?

Oh! I ain't much for all those un-natural smurfs! So I don't touch 'em!

And you, Chef Smurf?

You know... Hmm... When you smurf in the kitchen all day long, you don't really feel like eating your own cooking!

Hee hee!

Smurfette?

Let's just say I'm in the middle of a diet...

Fine! Fine! That confirms my suspicions!

I'll smurf a piece of this squash and analyze it in my laboratory!

Later...

I hope Papa Smurf will find an answer quickly!

Laboratory

All this because of a certain Smurf who--

I don't understand!

AAAAAH! Papa Smurf changed too! Run!

No, wait! There's surely an explanation!

How is this possible? It doesn't smurf with my theory!

But... But yes, of course!

Last night, after coming back from Gargamel's, I ate a little soup!

Now I just have to go smurf the others in the forest!

HEY! WHERE ARE YOU?

⇒Pfff!⇐... What will we smurf now that Papa Smurf has smurfed into a vegetable too?

Hey! Did you hear that?

It's Papa Smurf! He's gone in search of the others!

© Peyo 33

That's not good! Papa Smurf knows of our hiding place!

What?

Oh, no!

Maybe he's going to smurf them here and contaminate us!

We must smurf something!

What could we smurf so the other Smurfs go back to like before?

And what if Papa Smurf's right about the solutions? Remember, it all started after they were put on my garden, for smurf's sake!

But you know that Greedy Smurf hasn't been smurfed into a vegetable although he's eaten some!

Maybe Papa Smurf made a mistake about that! If we sprayed them with the same mixture, maybe they'd resmurf to like before?

Hmm... We could always try, but how do we smurf the solutions on all the Smurfs at once without getting close to them?

?

I have an idea! We'll spray them from above!

In the forest...

Where could they smurf? How will I find them?

?!

ZWIIIIIP

© Peyo

34

What the smurf--?! What smurfed?

WE GOT ONE!

That trap was a good idea, Handy Smurf!

Don't forget I'm the leader!

Let's smurf him! Let him become a vegetable too!

Huh? It's already done!

That's funny, he reminds me of someone!

If Papa Smurf were here, he'd smurf you a lesson! Since he isn't--

But I am Papa Smurf, you pack of two-legged veggie-smurfs! Smurf me down from here!

Papa Smurf is back!

YIPPEE!

Thanks, my friends! But let me speak! I must smurf you something important!

♪ Papa Smurf is back! Papa Smurf is back! ♪

BOP

?

Go on, Papa Smurf! Go on!

© Peyo

I've discovered it's the food that smurfed us into vegetables! Let's go back to the village. I'll find a way to cure us!

Yippee! We're returning to the village!

If it's the food, it's Farmer Smurf and Chef Smurf's fault!

When I catch them, I'll show them!

Meanwhile, at the village...

Nobody's here! We can go in!

Are you sure of what you're smurfing, Chef Smurf?

If you have a better idea, don't hold back!

I just hope that... ÷Gnnn!÷... Help me smurf the door!

CREEEEE

Heh heh! I knew Aerosmurf's* plane was still in the hangar!

And there's my big spray can that I smurf once a year for weeds!

Perfect! Go smurf the solutions Papa Smurf gave you for your garden and find a larger quantity in his laboratory!

36

*see THE SMURFS #16 "The Aerosmurf" or page 50.

Smurfette, if you wouldn't mind smurfing watch... In case the veggie-smurfs come back!

Of course!

Greedy Smurf, help me smurf the sprayer onto the plane. Afterwards, we'll push it out!

Here are the two flasks Papa Smurf smurfed to me. Quick, to the lab!

"Fungicide" and "natural fertilizer," that's them!

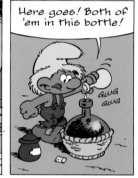

Here goes! Both of 'em in this bottle!

GLUG GLUG

I hope this'll do the job!

Hey! What the-- THE OTHERS! THE VEGGIE-SMURFS!

Look over there! Farmer Smurf!

It's his fault we're like this! Smurf him!

37

No, wait!

CHARGE!

© Peyo

Chef Smurf, I think we've forgotten Greedy Smurf!

?

?!

POC

LOOK OUT! SMURFETTE!

Hey, the bottle!

IIIIEEEE!

It's okay! Got 'er!

You have Smurfette?

Uh... No! The bottle!

We've got to smurf back for Smurfette!

Too late! I'm lifting off!

VVVVRRRRR

ASSASSINS!

?

IIIIEEEEE!
I'll be smurfed into a vegetable!

Have no fear, Smurfette! That won't happen to you. It's not contagious!

But what about you, Papa Smurf?

39

I'm like this because I ate some of the soup last night!

But Greedy Smurf smurfed some soup, too! Why is he still normal?

?

Greedy Smurf? For smurf's sake, I hadn't paid him any mind! Come here! Don't be scared!

It is strange! But my analyses were clear, it's because of the food! There must be a reason!

What are you smurfing there? Sarsaparilla?

Yep! It's like a dessert to me and it's good for digestion!

Did anyone smurf any sarsaparilla just before or after becoming a veggie-smurf?

No!

No!

Uh... no!

Nope!

No, and you?

Hmm, hmm! Interesting! What if...?

Hmm... I'll go smurf some tests! Nobody bother me!

Uh... Papa Smurf, I must smurf you something about Chef Smurf and Farmer Smurf!

What's wrong, Smurfette?

They have a plan to cure you! They want to spray on all of you a large quantity of the same stuff you gave to Farmer Smurf for his garden!

!

But that could be smurfly dangerous for all of us!

40

© Peyo

Our only chance is that sarsaparilla is the antidote! Otherwise, we'll be smurfed into vegetables permanently!

KOF KOF

YUM YUM

EUREKA! One bite is enough!

IIIEEE!

Look! They're acting weird!

⇒Buh!⇐

Greedy Smurf! Do you still have sarsaparilla leaves?

⇒Buh!⇐

?

KOF KOF

I have a few left in my pocket!

Smurf me half of it! Along with Smurfette, give the rest to any veggie-smurfs you run into!

Here, Jokey Smurf! Smurf this!

⇒Buh... I'm siiiiick... ⇒Yum!⇐ ⇒Yum!⇐

Yippee! I'm myself again! Who wants a gift?

You see anything in that pea soup?

Hey! Look out!

THE CHIMNEY?!

© Peyo

CRAC

42

WHAAA! HA! HA!

Hee Hee Hee!

What? What's wrong?

Why are you laughing?

AAAH!

Hey! You've gone back to normal!

It's thanks to me! My plan worked! The solutions we sprayed smurfed you back into Smurfs!

Not at all, Chef Smurf! You nearly smurfed great danger to all your friends!

Oh? Uh... We thought we were doing good!

Luckily, you know the antidote! You can smurf us back to our normal selves!

Yes, that's true!

Certainly, but I think staying in the form of vegetables for a while will smurf you a good lesson!

!

Later...

Your vegetables look good, Farmer Smurf! Too good to be true!

No, no! I assure you! I've smurfed only natural things on them!

It's been a week now, Papa Smurf! Couldn't we go back to being Smurfs again?

I'll think about it!

44

© Peyo

END

48

Welcome to the totally transformative twenty-sixth SMURFS graphic novel by Peyo, from Papercutz, those fast-food connoisseurs dedicated to publishing great graphic novels for all ages. I'm Jim Salad-crop, er, I mean, Jim Salicrup, the Chef Salad-loving Smurf-in-Chef, er, I mean, Chief. I'm here to share a few thoughts on Fruit and Veggie-Smurfs, share some exciting Smurf news, and tell you about another comics sensation we're sure you'll enjoy…

But first, let's talk about "Smurf Salad," shall we? While there are always folks around complaining how bad everything in the world has become, there are also many great things happening every day. Just in the field of nutrition, we know far more now than we ever have before. Back when I was a kid, we acted as if we could eat anything in moderation with little or no serious consequences. While my favorite breakfast cereal was *Kellogg's Rice Krispies*, with added banana slices, I did occasionally indulge in *Sugar Pops, Sugar Smacks*, and *Fruit Loops*, to name just a few. Obviously, with many of these cereals back then the major attraction was sugar, and as we realize today, too much (and exactly how much is too much?) sugar is just not healthy for you.

There was even an official Smurfs cereal during the run of the animated Smurfs cartoon show back in the 80s. *Smurf Berry Crunch* debuted on supermarket shelves in 1983, followed years later by *Smurf Magic Berries*. The advertising jingle was set to the tune of Tchaikovsky's *The Nutcracker Suite*…

> "*Smurf Berry Crunch* is fun to eat.
> A Smurfy fruity breakfast treat
> Made by Smurfs so happily.
> It tastes like crunchy Smurf Berries.
> It's berry-shaped and crispy too.
> In berry red and Smurfy blue."

See! How can you possibly resist that? The Smurfs themselves eat a much healthier diet, consisting mostly of various fruits and vegetables, although they do enjoy a Smurf baba (a rich cake soaked in rum and sugar syrup) every now and then. But that was then, and this is now. Although in "Smurf Salad" we never found out why the vegetables in Farmer Smurf's garden had gotten so bad in the first place, I think we learned that there can be awful side effects when tampering with Mother Nature's way of doing things.

And speaking of Mother Nature, it was recently announced that the Smurfs will be helping save the planet in two big ways. First, the Smurfs join the European Union's fight against ocean waste by taking part in the Global Beach Cleanup campaign in 140 countries around the world. Véronique Culliford, daughter of Peyo, joined João Aquiar Machado, director-general for fisheries and maritime affairs for the European Commission to sign the agreement. Sec-

ond, the Smurfs have joined the firefighters and national fire safety associations for the #Together4FireSafety campaign in Europe in order to improve fire safety in buildings for people. I guess that even includes Gargamel!

Papercutz is incredibly proud to be publishing THE SMURFS, not just because the characters are doing their part to save the planet, but because THE SMURFS are simply wonderful comics, the creation of Pierre Culliford, better known as Peyo. Recently, Papercutz through its Charmz imprint, has had the honor of publishing the work of yet another internationally acclaimed cartoonist, Mauricio de Sousa from Brazil. He created MONICA, a brash little girl with a plush blue bunny and her gang of friends. Charmz will be publishing the teenage version of this character in MONICA ADVENTURES. For more on this exciting comics event, see the bonus feature starting on page 58.

But back to THE SMURFS…as another extra bonus, we're representing the entire "Aerosmurf" story starting on the very next page. Why? Well, if you enjoyed "Smurf Salad," you already know the answer, and if you haven't, we don't want to offer any spoilers. And wasn't it spoiled veggies that started everything in this book? So, no spoilers, but be sure to look out for the next SMURFS graphic novel, and the all-new Smurfs animated series, both coming soon.

Smurf you later,

STAY IN TOUCH!

EMAIL: salicrup@papercutz.com
WEB: papercutz.com
TWITTER: @papercutzgn
INSTAGRAM: @papercutzgn
FACEBOOK: PAPERCUTZGRAPHICNOVELS
FANMAIL: Papercutz, 160 Broadway, Suite 700, East Wing, New York, NY 10038

THE AEROSMURF

by Peyo

Do you remember the Flying Smurf? (¹) Do you think he's forsaken his idea of rising up into the sky? Well, no! He's still thinking about it...

Ah! Icarus! What a lovely dream!

When suddenly, that morning...

Why, yes! How come I didn't smurf of that sooner?

I'll need Handy Smurf's help.

Handy Smurf, you have to smurf me a hand-to-smurf machine that'll smurf me into the smurf...

?

Hold on... I'll make you a blueprint...

Mmm, yeah... in theory, it ought to smurf, but I'd need some light wood, canvas, leather, rubber, screws, springs...

I'll look for all that!

And late into the night...

When will that racket be over?

BING
THWOOF
BING
TZEEEEEE
DZEEEEE
BANG
BANG

(¹) From THE SMURFS #1, of course!

50

The next morning...

HEY!

Everybody come! Check out the marvelous invention I smurfed last night!

What's that smurf?

It's an aerosmurf! A machine that's going to let me fly, thanks to its wings and a big rubber band that'll smurf the propeller!

Well, my smurf...

Do you really think that'll smurf?

Heavier-than-air!

He's going to bust his smurf!

Obviously!

Okay, I'll wind up my machine!

GR?

GRRRR

Watch out! Smurf back! I'm smurfing for take-off!

Me, I don't like take-offs!

FRRRRRRR

2

It works! I'M FLYING! I'M FLYING!

Bravo! It smurfs!

He got something heavier-than-air to fly!

I said it would smurf!

52

54

57

monica
Adventures

Meet Monica.

She is fierce, confident, and super strong. She won't put up with anyone teasing her or her friends. She's always been like that…

Monica's first appearance in Jimmy Five's newspaper strip on March 3rd, 1963. Even if you don't speak Portuguese, you can see the start of this comic rivalry.

Charmz, is proud to publish Monica's adolescent adventures in the United States and Canada for the first time. Monica and her gang have been friends for years, since childhood. Now, join Monica and her gang of friends as they take on all the ups and downs of high school life including dating, social media, crushes, gossip, or just finding the cash to enjoy a night at the movies.

There's a lot to love about Monica. We asked celebrated comics writer Gail Simone for a blurb announcing Monica's arrival on the North American comics scene and here's what she wrote: "The international phenomenon comes to America, with all the charm, fun, and cuteness intact. Monica's here, gang!"

As Gail said, Monica is an international phenomenon. For example, Monica and J-Five have hobnobbed with *Astro Boy* and other classic manga characters such as *Kimba the White Lion* and *Princess Knight*. Mauricio de Sousa, Monica's creator, was a personal friend of their creator, the late master of manga, Osamu Tezuka. He even has a cameo in MONICA ADVENTURES #1!

Osamu's cameo.

Not to be outdone, Monica then helped save the universe by teaming up with none other than the *Justice League*! That's right! Monica has met *Wonder Woman, Superman, Batman,* and all the rest. These adventures are only available in Brazil so far, but who knows what the future may bring?

MONICA is actually one of the first ladies of comics. Created by legendary Brazilian cartoonist Mauricio de Sousa in 1963, her comic adventures as a young, super-strong girl in her neighborhood have taken most of the world by storm since her debut. Monica has been translated to 14 languages and has appeared in 40 countries and counting!

CLASS IS OUT EARLY, I GUESS. SEE THAT?

SEE HOW ESSENTIAL THESE *SITES* ARE?

ESSENTIAL, YEAH...

... FOR THOSE THAT LIKE MEDDLING IN OTHER PEOPLE'S LIVES.

FINE, *HUN!* ACT LIKE A SAINT ALL YOU WANT, OKAY?

I SAW YOU LIKE THAT POST FROM YOUR PHONE!

U-UM... IT'S JUST... WELL...

LET'S GET ONE THING STRAIGHT, OKAY?

EVEN MO' GIGGLED A BIT.

Now, thanks to resident Monica fan, managing editor Jeff Whitman, Charmz is bringing Monica to the USA and Canada. "In Brazil, Monica is everywhere you look, from diapers to headlining Comic Cons that rival the big ones here. She is the bestselling brand in Brazil and it is virtually impossible to avoid her influence there," said Jeff. "Her comics are pure enjoyment, with a robust cast of colorful characters you can identify with, zany plots spoofing or parodying all genres, and with a gentle reminder of how it is to be a kid. She is timeless. I knew her adventures as a teenager, presented in a manga-like style, would be perfect for North American audiences.

There's humor, drama, and a whole lot of heart. It is an impressive repertoire that we are just beginning to scratch the surface of. Creator Mauricio de Sousa, his daughter (the real-life inspiration behind Monica!), and the whole studio in Brazil has welcomed Charmz and

MONICA creator, Mauricio de Sousa, with Monica fan and Charmz editor, Jeff Whitman.

me with open arms. Bringing these wonderful comics to the United States and Canada was the next logical step for Monica and her friends!"

Monica and her gang aren't kids anymore in MONICA ADVENTURES. But things haven't changed much as Monica got older. Jimmy-Five now goes by J-Five but still gets tongue-tied around Monica. Instead of teasing her, he pines for her, and hopes to be as successful as her one day. Maggy tries to eat healthier these days, and Smudge has accepted the necessity of a shower, but old habits die hard!

Nancy and Sluggo, Lois and Clark, Jane and Tarzan, Monica and Jimmy Five...some classic comics couples.

Monica first appeared as a young girl in the comics, always running her block as the girl-in-charge. Super-strong, with a short temper and a rather short stature, she was the perfect target for the conniving, but lovable, Jimmy Five (the five stands for the amount of hairs on his head), and his best friend Smudge, who is certifiably afraid of water, to come up with all sorts of maniacal and "infallible" plans to usurp Monica as the leader of their group of friends. Plans, which Monica usually can thwart with her eyes closed and some help from her blue plush rabbit (that doubles as a dangerous projectile), Samson. Add in Monica's best friend, the always-famished Maggy, and some other unforgettable and relatable neighborhood kids and the recipe (calm down, Maggy, not that kind of recipe!) for fun is endless.

J-Five and Smudge are bigger comicbook nerds than anyone we know!

Already picked up the first two volumes of MONICA ADVENTURES and want more Monica now without having to take an intensive Portuguese class? Head over to YouTube and check out the "Monica Toy Official" channel to see hundreds of videos of Monica and friends. The best part? The videos have no words! Monica's comedic timing needs no explanation! While you're there, tell them your friends at Charmz sent you!